Stories of Gnomes & Goblins

Christopher Rawson

Adapted by Lesley Sims

Illustrated by
Stephen Cartwright

Reading Consultant: Alison Kelly
University of Surrey Roehampton

Contents

Chapter 1

The lazy gnome

Harold was a happy farmer, until the day a gnome arrived.

"This place looks good!" said the gnome. "I think I'll stay." Harold couldn't get rid of him.

At first, the gnome helped on the farm. But one day he went on strike and refused to do anything. That wasn't all.

"From now on, I want half of everything you grow," he shouted at Harold.

Harold didn't like that at all. So he agreed but decided he would trick the gnome.

OK, you can have half the next crop. Do you want the top or bottom half?

Umm, the bottom half.

That spring, Harold planted wheat in his fields. At harvest time, Harold took the top of the wheat and had sacks full of grain. The gnome got stalks.

Grr! You tricked me! I meant half of the field.

"Next year, I'll take the top of the crop," said the gnome. So, Harold planted turnips.

At harvest time, Harold had piles of turnips. The gnome got the top of the plant: leaves.

The gnome was very angry. "Next year, grow wheat again," he shouted. "You can cut half the field and I'll cut half. Whoever finishes first can take all the wheat."

A race?

Yes! And I'm small and fast, so I'll win.

When the wheat was ready to cut, Harold went to the village blacksmith. He had a plan, but it needed lots of thin iron rods.

The night before the race,
Harold crept out to his field.
He stuck the thin iron rods
among the wheat, on the
gnome's half of the field.

Next day, Harold's scythe swished through the wheat easily. But the gnome's scythe kept hitting the rods.

Every time the gnome tried
to cut the wheat, his scythe hit
a rod. Soon it would not cut at
all. The gnome was so angry,
he shouted at Harold.

In a temper, he threw down
the scythe and stormed off.
Harold never saw him again.

Chapter 2

Goblin Hill

Jessy was skipping in the sun when she heard a tiny, tiny cry.

"Help me! Please, help me!"

13

When she looked down,
there was a fairy, stuck in a
spider's web.

Jessy could hardly believe
her eyes. Gently, she lifted the
fairy from the web.

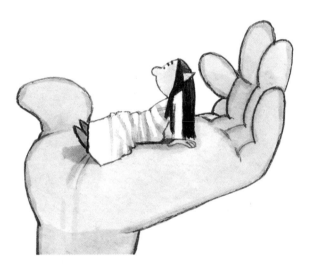

"Thank you, thank you!" cried the
fairy. "I was going to Goblin Hill for
a party. Would you like to come?"

15

Jessy's gran had told her
stories about Goblin Hill.
Not once had Jessy imagined
goblins actually lived there.

But, now she looked closely,
she saw a door.

"Imagine going into the
hill!" said Jessy, but she was
far too big...

...until the fairy tapped her on the toe.

The fairy opened the door and led Jessy inside.

They arrived in the middle of a goblin parade.

"It's to celebrate the return of Prince Kester," said the fairy.

18

Prince Kester was very excited to meet Jessy. He had never seen a girl up close before.

He asked the goblin choir
to sing a song just for Jessy.
The royal band tried to play
along, but they kept playing
wrong notes.

All together
now... Higher...
higher!

"And now, the Balancing Elves!" said the king. Jessy clapped loudly. But they were more like Falling Elves.

The Balancing Elves were followed by the Juggling Pixies. They were even funnier than the clowns.

Finally, everyone sat down
to a huge picnic in
the shade of a
lollipop
tree.

Let the feast begin!

"I must go," said Jessy, at last. "My mother will wonder where I am."

"Don't worry," said the king. "Time stands still here."

23

Jessy ran down the tunnel
and rolled out of the door.
Outside, the grass was a
jungle. Jessy was still the
size of a bee.

But, as she stood up, Jessy shot to her usual size. She looked back at the hill. The door was nowhere to be seen.

Jessy shook her head. What a fantastic adventure, but would her friends ever believe her?

Chapter 3

A magic bridge

Jack had been walking for weeks. Today, the end of his journey was in sight. "The city of Oxford!" he cried.

As the sun was setting, he reached a bridge on the edge of the city. He was too tired to walk another step.

Ah, it's good to rest my feet.

Jack took some straw from his sack to make a bed. He lay down on the bridge. Soon, he was snoring gently.

But Jack had fallen asleep on
a pixie bridge. In the middle of
the night, the pixies arrived.

They flew down and pulled
pieces of straw from his bed.
One pulled too hard. He woke
Jack up.

Jack watched the pixies fly
away on the straw. He wished
he could follow them.

All at once, he could!

After a long flight,
they landed on
a chimney.
One by one,
the pixies
flew inside.
Jack followed.

He landed in an enormous cellar, filled with partying pixies. One gave him a silver cup full of a fruity drink.

A band played and they danced all night. But, as the sun rose, everyone vanished. Jack fell asleep...

...and woke up back on the bridge. He thought it had been a dream, until he saw the silver cup.

Jack tried to sell the cup to buy some breakfast. But the shopkeeper was horrified.

"Thief! Police!" yelled the man. Jack turned and fled. He didn't get very far.

Jack was taken to a judge who told him off.

"You slept on the pixies' bridge?" cried the judge. "Why didn't you say? You're free to go. Just be careful where you sleep from now on."

Chapter 4

Willo the Wisp

Every day, on his way home from school, James saw a strange light. It shone far away over the marshes.

When he asked his mother about it, she turned pale.

"That's the candle of Willo the Wisp," she said. "Keep away!"

If you follow his light, you'll lose your way in the marshes and never come back.

For a whole week, James tried not to think about the light. But one night he just couldn't sleep. He crept from his bedroom and headed out onto the marsh.

A frightened frog croaked at him as he went by.

"Go back or Willo the Wisp will get you!" it warned. James went on.

A worried owl hooted at him as he went by.

"Go back or Willo the Wisp will get you!" it warned. James went on.

"If he catches you," called the owl, "blow out his candle. That breaks the spell."

James followed the light, deeper and deeper into the dangerous marsh. The light was getting closer...

James grabbed the candle
and blew
it out in
one puff.

As the flame went out,
James found he could move.
He turned and ran for home.

He ran past the worried owl. "Thank you! You saved my life," he told the owl.

He ran past the frightened frog. "I wish I'd listened to you," he said to the frog. "I'll never visit the marshes again."

Back home, he scrambled up the tree to his bedroom.

Safe under the covers, James breathed a sigh of relief. He put Willo the Wisp's candle by his bed.

After that, whenever he felt curious about something, he looked at the candle. One look and his curiosity went out like a light.

Try these other books in
Series One:

Witches: Three tales about witches: one
who loses her broomstick, one who loses
her temper, and one who loses her
cool with a clever farmer.

The Dinosaurs Next Door: Mr. Puff's
house is full of amazing things. Best of
all are the dinosaur eggs – until
they begin to hatch...

Wizards: One wizard looks after orphans,
one sells cures, and one must stop a band
of robbers from taking the last sack
of gold in the castle.

The Monster Gang: The Monster Gang
is together for their first meeting in
the treehouse. But one of the
monsters hides a secret.

Designed by
Katarina Dragoslavić

First published in 2003 by Usborne Publishing Ltd., Usborne House,
83-85 Saffron Hill, London EC1N 8RT, England. www.usborne.com
Copyright © 2003, 1980 Usborne Publishing Ltd.